UNM
GALLUP

Zollinger Library

GERONIMO

Young Warrior

Illustrated by Meryl Henderson

GERONIMO

Young Warrior

by George Edward Stanley

ALADDIN PAPERBACKS

New York   London   Toronto   Sydney   Singapore

First Aladdin Paperbacks edition September 2001
Text copyright © 2001 by George Edward Stanley
Illustrations copyright © 2001 by Meryl Henderson

Aladdin Paperbacks
An imprint of Simon & Schuster Children's Publishing Division
1230 Avenue of the Americas
New York, NY 10020

The text of this book was set in Adobe Garamond
Designed by Lisa Vega
Manufactured in the United States of America.

10

Cataloging-in-Publication data available from the Library of Congress.

ISBN-13: 978-0-689-84455-3
ISBN-10: 0-689-84455-7
0614 OFF

Illustrations

CONTENTS

GERONIMO

Young Warrior

He Who Yawns

Chappo hurried down the dusty path toward the center of the Bedonkohe Apache village. He was going to the tepee of Juana and Taklishim. There was someone inside he was eager to meet.

Along the way, Chappo passed other tepees and even some brush-covered wicki-ups. The wickiups belonged to members of the Nednai Apache tribe who were visiting from Mexico. All Apaches lived in wickiups in times of war, because they had to move fast. But the Apaches were not warring with

1

the Mexicans now. So most of the Bedonkohe Apaches in the village lived in tepees.

Chappo thought Juana and Taklishim's tepee was the most beautiful one in the village. It was made of deer and antelope hides and decorated with many colorful designs.

Juana and Taklishim were very important members of the tribe. Taklishim's father, Mahko, had once been a great chief.

All morning among the people of the village there had been excitement. Juana and Taklishim had a new baby. Chappo slipped quietly inside the tepee and looked around. "Where is my new brother?" he asked. "I would like to see him."

Juana and Taklishim smiled. They knew that the new baby was not really Chappo's brother. He was only a cousin. But to Apaches, other relatives were sometimes called brothers and sisters.

"Here he is," Juana said. She held up the baby for Chappo to see.

Chappo looked into the baby's wrinkled brown face and smiled at him. The baby yawned. Chappo kept smiling. The baby kept yawning.

"What will you call him?" Chappo asked.

"We will call him Goyahkla," Taklishim said. "He Who Yawns."

Chappo laughed. That is a good name, he thought. He had never seen a baby who yawned so much. Chappo wondered if his new brother would be weak and lazy. He wondered if he would want to sleep all the time instead of play the games that Apache boys played.

But Chappo quickly banished these thoughts. He knew it was wrong for Apaches to think bad thoughts about one another.

Chappo need not have worried about Goyahkla's future. But on that hot, dusty day in 1829 no one in the tepee could know that this name would never fit the new baby. When the baby grew up, he would become famous as Geronimo.

Chappo turned and left the tepee. For several minutes he stood outside the entrance and looked up to the peaks of the Gila Mountains. His heart was full. New life had come to his village. Even if his new brother did turn out to be lazy and to sleep all the time, Chappo wanted to sing out his happiness. He quickly decided what he needed to do.

There was one special peak on which he felt closest to Usen, the Life Giver of the Apaches. He would go there and pray that his new brother would live a long and happy life.

As Chappo started down toward the Gila River, which he had to cross to get to the peak, he passed Ishton. Ishton was the daughter of Juana and Taklishim. She had gone to the river to get water in which to bathe the new baby.

"I am going to the top of the mountain," Chappo said. He didn't have to tell Ishton which one. "I am going to pray to Usen to keep Goyahkla safe from the evil spirits."

5

Ishton smiled. "Chappo, I hope you will also pray to White Painted Woman and to Child of Water," she said. "They are good spirits and will keep Goyahkla safe, too."

"Yes, I will, Ishton," Chappo assured her.

Ishton smiled at him again. She had called him by his name, which meant he could not refuse her request. Apaches did not usually call people by their names unless the occasion was very special.

Ishton watched as Chappo continued toward the river. Then she hurried on to the tepee where her mother and father and her new brother were waiting for her.

When Ishton entered the tepee, she found Juana nursing Goyahkla. Ishton knew her mother would do this until her brother was able to eat solid food. Then he would be given only the best meats and vegetables. Nobody in the village would complain about this, either. Apache children were both wanted and loved. In fact, they were treated almost royally, because when there were lots of children in a village, it meant that the tribe would not die out.

It didn't matter to Apache parents if their child was a girl or a boy. Even though boys went to live with their wives' families when they married, they could still hunt and fish to help provide food for the people of the village before the marriage took place. Boys could also become great warriors and make their families proud of them.

Girls, when they married, stayed in their village. Their husbands came to live with them. That meant that an Apache family gained a son who could help provide things that the family needed.

"My daughter, will you go with your father to speak to the medicine man about making Goyahkla's *tosch*?" Juana asked when she saw Ishton.

"Oh, yes, Mother!" Ishton replied. "It will be an honor."

The *tosch* was the Apache cradle board. It was a very important part of Apache childhood. When he was four days old, Goyahkla would be put in it with much ceremony. The whole village would help the family celebrate. There would be lots of delicious food to eat, too. After the ceremony, Goyahkla would be taken out of the cradle board and would not be put back in it until he was a month old.

Ishton followed her father to a tepee beside the Gila River. Inside, they found Teo, the old medicine man. "We have come to ask you to make a cradle board for Goyahkla," Taklishim said. "I will pay you well."

Teo reached behind him and brought forth the most beautiful cradle board Ishton had ever seen. It was made of split yucca boughs. They had been cut thin and scraped until they were very smooth. A willow branch formed the frame of the cradle board. At the head there was a roof made of stretched buckskin to protect the baby's head from rain or sun. Goyahkla would lie on a mattress and a pillow stuffed with wild mustard grass. Ishton wondered how much this cradle board would cost her father.

"I knew you would come. I have already made the cradle board and blessed it," the medicine man said. "You always bring me the best meat and skins from the hunts. The cradle board will cost you nothing more." Teo handed the cradle board to Taklishim.

Ishton let out a short gasp. Teo was truly a medicine man. He must have known what she had been thinking.

"You honor my family," Taklishim said. "Thank you."

With a baby in the tepee, the daily life of Ishton's family changed a lot, but Ishton quickly adapted to the new routine. It was her duty to help take care of her brother. She felt even more grown up now that she had been given this responsibility.

One day, Ishton followed Juana to the

banks of the Gila River. Juana took Goyahkla out of the cradle board and put him down on a blanket under a big tree. "You must watch him carefully," she told Ishton. "You must make sure no harm comes to him."

"I will, Mother," Ishton said.

But Goyahkla didn't stay on the blanket very long after Juana left. With what sounded like giggles, he rolled off of the blanket and onto the ground.

Instead of picking him up and putting him back on the blanket, though, Ishton let Goyahkla roll around in the dirt. According to Apache ritual, she made sure he rolled in all four directions: east, west, north, and south.

It was an Apache custom to do this in the village where a person was born. Later in life, whenever Goyahkla returned to his village in the Gila Mountains, beside the Gila River, he would roll on the ground in all four directions. All Apaches did this to celebrate their connection to the earth.

The First Moccasins

When Goyahkla was four months old, Juana awakened Nah-dos-te, another one of Goyahkla's sisters, and said, "This morning, we will give Goyahkla his earrings to help him grow faster. I want you to help me with the ceremony."

"Yes, Mother," Nah-dos-te said. She considered this a great honor.

Nah-dos-te left the tepee and walked down to the banks of the Gila River. There she found what she was looking for: two small rocks that were flat and smooth. She took them back to the village and threw them into the campfire. After several minutes she removed the rocks with a couple of sticks. She put them in a small piece of deerskin and carried them back to the tepee. Goyahkla was lying on an antelope blanket. Juana was at his side. Nah-dos-te squatted down beside them.

"Put one of the stones under his left ear," Juana said.

Nah-dos-te did as she was asked. She was surprised when Goyahkla didn't make a sound.

Juana took a sharp thorn and punctured the baby's earlobe. Then she took a turquoise earring that had been made especially for Goyahkla by one of the women in the village. She put it into his ear. Then Juana and Nah-dos-te repeated the ceremony with Goyahkla's right ear.

"They are beautiful," Nah-dos-te said when both earrings were in Goyahkla's ears.

"They will make him hear better and grow

faster," Juana said. She smiled at Nah-dos-te. "That is what your earrings have done for you," she added.

One morning, several months later, Juana said to Ishton, "Goyahkla is restless. I think it is time for him to leave the *tosch*."

So Goyahkla was taken out of the cradle board and allowed to crawl all over the camp. Sometimes, Ishton and Chappo would chase him. This caused Goyahkla to giggle and made him crawl even faster.

"He looks as if he is searching for animal tracks on the ground," Chappo said one day as Goyahkla was crawling from one tepee to another.

"Yes, he does," said Ishton. "Someday he will be a great hunter."

When Goyahkla was a year old he crawled to the edge of a tepee and suddenly stood up. He balanced himself with one hand against the side of the tepee and took a few wobbly steps. He stood for a moment. Ishton was sure she saw surprise in his eyes at what he had just done. She ran to find Juana and Taklishim. "Mother! Father!" she shouted. "Come quickly! It's Goyahkla!"

Juana dropped the gourd of water she was holding. She and Taklishim ran to follow Ishton. "Has something terrible happened to him?" Juana cried. The loss of her child would be unbearable. The whole tribe would mourn.

When the three of them reached the edge of the village, they saw a crowd. They pushed through to the middle.

There was Goyahkla. He was running around in circles and squealing with laughter.

"Oh!" Juana cried. She was so relieved that nothing bad had happened to Goyahkla that she could say nothing else.

Taklishim beamed proudly.

That evening, Juana and Taklishim went again to see Teo, the medicine man. He would help them prepare for the ceremony of putting on Goyahkla's first moccasins. There would be songs, prayers, and dancing. Again, there would be lots of food to eat. Everyone in the village would be invited.

Juana asked Bi-ya-neta, her best friend, who lived in the tepee next to her, to make Goyahkla's buckskin outfit. Bi-ya-neta had lost a boy child a few months earlier. Juana thought it would make her happy to be part of Goyahkla's ceremony.

Finally, one evening, just before the sun set, Teo came to Taklishim and Juana's tepee. "There will be a full moon tonight," he said. "It is time to celebrate Goyahkla's first steps."

"We are ready," Taklishim said.

Juana dressed Goyahkla in his new buckskin outfit. It fit perfectly. Bi-ya-neta had made it with great care.

All of the tribe got dressed in their finest clothes and put feathers in their hair.

Everyone walked to the center of the village,

15

where a huge bonfire had been built. Long blankets of antelope hides had been laid end-to-end on the ground, just a short distance from the fire. The blankets were covered with food.

Ishton couldn't remember ever having seen so much food at one time. There were pumpkins, beans, corn, and buffalo meat. There were walnuts, acorns, juniper berries, piñon nuts, and wild onions. It made Ishton happy that the people in their village thought so highly of her family that they would prepare such a feast for her brother.

Chappo came to stand beside her. "I have fasted all day," he whispered. "I can eat half of what you see."

Ishton grinned at him. She took his hand, and together they sat down next to the rest of the family.

Goyahkla was sitting in Taklishim's lap. Juana and Nah-dos-te sat on Taklishim's right. Chappo and Ishton sat on Taklishim's left.

Teo stood up and faced the crowd. "Tonight, we Apaches celebrate the child Goyahkla. We hope he will continue to be strong and healthy. That will be our prayer to Usen," he told the people of the village. "We also celebrate the child Goyahkla tonight because Child of Water, when he first walked, had a similar ceremony." Then the medicine man sat down.

The other young girls of the village began serving the food. Usually, Ishton and Nah-dos-te helped, but tonight, as sisters of Goyahkla, they were honored guests.

When all the members of the village had eaten until they were full, the dancing began. The first dance gave thanks to Child of Water for Goyahkla's first steps. The dance told a story: All life was a path that every Apache walked down. All Apaches must follow the path in the same way Child of Water did.

This dance was followed by ritual songs and other dances. At sunrise, the singing and the dancing stopped, and the people sat on the ground, exhausted, but still excited about what was to come.

The medicine man took the sleeping Goyahkla from Taklishim's arms and lifted him up toward the sky. He turned Goyahkla toward each of the four directions. North. South. East. West. He did this four times.

When he finished, the medicine man handed Goyahkla back to Taklishim. This was the signal for two men from the village to place a long blanket of white buckskin in front of the medicine man. They sprinkled pollen on it. The medicine man walked through the pollen, making footprints.

Taklishim handed Goyahkla back to Teo. The medicine man put Goyahkla down on the buckskin and led him through the pollen footprints.

"Usen, protect your child Goyahkla," the medicine man prayed at each step. "Give him good fortune in life."

The medicine man led Goyahkla through

the pollen footprints four times. Then he walked him clockwise around the buckskin four times.

When he finished this, Teo stood on the blanket of white buckskin with Goyahkla by his side. Everyone in the village passed by. Each person reached down, swiped at the pollen with his or her fingers, and marked Goyahkla's hair and face and arms with it.

When they had finished marking Goyahkla with pollen, there were still more songs and dancing. Finally, the medicine man laid Goyahkla's first moccasins on the ground in front of him. Juana and Taklishim knelt in front of their son.

"Moccasins!" Goyahkla cried. "Feet!"

Juana put one of the moccasins on Goyahkla's left foot. Taklishim put the other one on Goyahkla's right foot.

Goyahkla started walking through the admiring crowd. Suddenly, he began jumping up and down. Then he ran to Ishton's arms. "Ishton! Ishton!" he cried. He pointed to his moccasins. "Pretty!"

"Yes, they are pretty, Goyahkla," Ishton said. She patted Goyahkla's head and caressed his long black hair, knowing that in the spring there would be a haircutting ceremony to celebrate both Goyahkla's growth and the growth of all living things.

Getting in Trouble

While Goyahkla was growing up, the Apaches were at peace. They had even begun to trade with their enemies, the Mexicans. It would be several years before this peace would end. It would be several more years after that before the Apaches and the white Americans would be at war with one another.

When Goyahkla wasn't playing with friends his own age in the village, he would often hide and watch Ishton and Nah-dos-te as they helped their mother gather firewood and food from the wild plants that grew in the area around the village. Goyahkla missed the times when Ishton and Nah-dos-te played with him all the time. But his sisters were older now. They were expected to do their share of work in the village before they could play with him.

Goyahkla knew that, as a boy, he would never do what his sisters did. He would never carry water from the spring, help build new wickiups, or cook the meals for the village. That was the work of women.

When Goyahkla was nine years old, word came to the village that some Mexicans had been seen in the area south of the Gila River. Many people started to worry that the peace between the Apaches and the Mexicans might be coming to an end. Taklishim and some of the other warriors decided to find out why the Mexicans were there.

"The time has come for you to help me, Goyahkla," Taklishim said one day. "Go to the corral and get my horse ready for me to ride."

"Yes, Father," Goyahkla said proudly.

In his heart, Goyahkla knew he would miss the carefree days when all he did was play with the other children in the village. But he also knew that today he was starting the journey toward becoming a man. Preparing their fathers' horses was a coming-of-age ritual for all Apache boys.

Goyahkla ran toward the corral at the edge of the village where the horses were kept. His father owned several horses that had been either captured or traded from the Mexicans. Taklishim's favorite horse was called Cactus. The horse had gotten his name because his favorite meal was the insides of the cactus plants that grew nearby.

Before Goyahkla reached the corral, he stopped and cut off several pieces of cactus. His father's horse was running toward him by the time he reached the corral fence. "You can smell it, can't you?" Goyahkla said.

He let Cactus eat the pieces of cactus from

his hand. Cactus's tongue tickled his fingers. Goyahkla loved to rub Cactus's smooth nose. He didn't think there was anything softer than the nose of a horse.

"Now it's time to get you ready," Goyahkla said to Cactus. "Father is going to ride you out of the village today."

With him, Goyahkla had a soft antelope blanket that his father used as a saddle, and a leather bridle that Goyahkla's grandfather, the great Chief Mahko, had taken from the dead horse of a Spaniard.

Goyahkla saw that some of his friends weren't putting anything on the backs of their fathers' horses. Some Apaches preferred to ride bareback. "This is not good," Taklishim had told Goyahkla. "This sometimes causes raw places on the horse's back, and he can't be used." Still others were putting Mexican saddles on their fathers' horses.

Goyahkla led Cactus out of the corral to his family's tepee. He stood at the opening, holding the reins, until his father came out a few minutes later.

"I may be gone for several moons, Goyahkla," Taklishim said. "We need to find out what the Mexicans are doing on our land."

Goyahkla could hear the concern in his father's voice. "I will look after my mother and my sisters," he assured his father.

Taklishim placed his hand on the top of Goyahkla's head. "You are a good son, Goyahkla," he said. "When I return, I will let you hold my arrows while I tie the feathers on them."

"Thank you, Father," Goyahkla said. It filled his heart that his father thought he was ready to do this.

Juana was standing together with Ishton and Nah-dos-te at the entrance to the tepee. Goyahkla had never seen such a look of sadness on his mother's face.

Taklishim nodded at Juana. Then he mounted Cactus. Goyahkla handed him the reins. Without looking back, Taklishim started out of the village. He was followed by the other warriors.

When Goyahkla turned, his mother and his sisters had gone back into the tepee. Goyahkla knew his mother was worried that something might happen while his father was gone. He had never really thought about that before. Goyahkla loved to hear the stories about how the Apaches chased the Mexicans away when the Mexicans tried to attack Apache villages. He especially liked to hear the stories of how the Apaches, to punish the Mexicans, raided their villages and took what they wanted. But they were just stories then. Now his father had gone off to see what the Mexicans wanted. For the first time in his life, Goyahkla realized that these stories could be real.

But life went on in the Apache village, so Goyahkla didn't have much time to think about what his father was doing. The next morning his mother said, "Today, we go on top of the mountain. It is time that I teach you how to pray to Usen."

Ishton handed Goyahkla a large gourd with water which she had drawn especially from the Gila River for the trip. They would not take any food. Their fast would prove to Usen that they were serious about what they were doing.

Juana and Goyahkla started out of the village. They crossed the Gila River and started up the side of the mountain. A gentle breeze was blowing and, although it was very warm, the air cooled Goyahkla's skin.

As they climbed the mountain, Juana taught Goyahkla the legends of the Apache people. She told him about Earth Woman and Thunder People. She told him about White Painted Woman and Child of Water. She told him about Water Beings and Controller of Water. She told him about the Mountain People and the Mountain Spirits.

The one story Goyahkla wanted to hear most, though, was about Coyote. He sounded like a formidable foe. "Coyote is a trickster," Juana said. "All the wicked things that man does Coyote did first."

Goyahkla shivered just thinking about what would happen if he encountered Coyote.

Juana also told him tales of the sun and the sky, the moon and the stars, the clouds and the storms. After a couple of hours they reached the place on the mountain that was most sacred to Juana. Juana showed Goyahkla how to kneel. Then she knelt beside him. "When you pray to Usen," Juana said, "you pray for strength, health, wisdom, and protection."

Goyahkla thought for a minute. "Mother, should I pray to Usen to protect Father against the Mexicans? If they try to kill him, should I ask Usen to help him kill them first?"

"No, my son," Juana replied. "We never pray for Usen's help against others."

"Why not, Mother?" Goyahkla asked.

"It is not the Apache way," Juana said. "If you have something against another person, you must take vengeance yourself."

Goyahkla would never forget his mother's words as they knelt on the side of the mountain above their village. When he became a man and had to protect himself and his family from attacks by Mexicans and by American settlers as they moved west, he would always know that he was doing what Usen expected him to do.

When Goyahkla and Juana got back to the village, Juana went to where Ishton and Nahdos-te were helping a newly arrived family of Nednai Apaches build a wickiup. They would live in the wickiup for the next few months while they visited with relatives and friends in the village.

With his father gone, Goyahkla felt a sense of independence he had never felt before. Unfortunately, it started getting him in trouble. When his mother asked him to help some of the old men in the village, he refused. So Juana splashed cold water in Goyahkla's face. But that punishment didn't do any good.

When Goyahkla's sisters asked him to find some sharp rocks to help them scrape buffalo hides, he refused. So they ignored him for several days. But that punishment didn't work, either.

Finally, Juana had had enough. She knew what she had to do to stop this kind of behavior. She went to the tepee of an old friend. "Goyahkla doesn't obey me," she said. "He refuses to listen."

"I know what to do," the old friend said. "I shall come to your tepee tonight just as the fire is almost out."

That night, just as Goyahkla drifted off to sleep, a voice shouted, "Where is that bad boy I heard about when I was way underground? I have come to carry him away with me!"

Goyahkla's eyes opened wide. Hovering over him was a humpbacked figure with long, tangled hair. His face was as dark as soot. His clothing was torn and hung in strips from his body. He also carried a huge basket over his shoulders.

Goyahkla started crying. He knew who this creature was. He had heard many tales about him. He was the evil monster who punished bad Apache children. "Please do not take me underground with you," Goyahkla cried. "I promise to obey my family and the elders of the village."

"If you promise that, then I will not take you away this time," the man said. "But if you break your word, I shall return!"

It took Goyahkla a while to go back to sleep after the monster left, but he finally did. When he awakened the next morning, he vowed again that he would never disobey his family or the elders of the village.

Goyahkla kept his promise, too. Whenever

his mother or his sisters or the old men of the village asked for his help, he gave it willingly. Many times, he even helped them without being asked. In fact, by the time Taklishim and the other Apache warriors returned safely to the village, everyone seemed to have forgotten about Goyahkla's bad behavior.

Goyahkla was glad. He would never want to lose his father's respect.

Becoming a Man

Goyahkla had been awake for several hours. He couldn't sleep, but he knew he had to be quiet so as not to awaken the other members of his family. He wished the sun would rise, so everyone would get up. Ishton and Nah-dos-te had promised to take him to the high mesa today. They were going to slide down it in a toboggan that Goyahkla's friend Alchise had made for them. It would almost be like the old days, when they played together all the time.

"Will you come with us?" Goyahkla had asked Alchise the night before.

Alchise shook his head. "I have other things to do," he replied.

"What things?" Goyahkla asked.

Alchise shrugged.

"Well, can't you do whatever you have to do after we slide down the mesa?" Goyahkla said.

"No! I will soon be a man," Alchise said. "I'm too old to play with girls." With that, he turned and stalked off.

How could that be? Goyahkla wondered. Alchise was only a few months older than he was.

Alchise's words gave Goyahkla a funny feeling. He had never thought before that there was anything wrong with playing with girls. He and his sisters had always played together.

They put on earrings, necklaces, and bracelets made of grass and pine needles. They played house. Goyahkla even helped Ishton and Nah-dos-te make cradle boards for their dolls. Ishton and Nah-dos-te helped

Goyahkla make balls of clay, which he then put on the fork of a twig and slung at birds. Several times he killed enough birds to make meals for his family.

In summer, Goyahkla and his sisters swam together in the Gila River. What was wrong with that?

"Are you ready, Brother?"

Goyahkla turned to see Ishton and Nah-dos-te. Nah-dos-te was holding the toboggan. It was made out of a long piece of cowhide that had dried hard in the sun. In the front there were buckskin loops for your feet so you wouldn't fall off.

"Yes," Goyahkla replied. But what Alchise had said to him had taken some of the fun out of what they were going to do. Goyahkla stood looking at his sisters.

"What is wrong with you, Brother?" Nah-dos-te demanded. "Help me carry this toboggan to the mesa."

Goyahkla took a deep breath. "Yes, Sister,"

he said. He didn't care what Alchise thought. He was going to have a good time today playing with his sisters.

The three of them left the village and headed east toward the two mesas. To Goyahkla, the mesas looked like mountains that had their tops cut off. He always liked to climb them. Sometimes, he liked to race across the smooth, flat top toward the edge and see if he could stop before he went off.

"That's a crazy game," Ishton had told him many times before. "If you don't stop doing that, we won't bring you next time." But Goyahkla didn't stop, and his sisters still brought him with them.

The three of them finally reached the side of the mesa that had the best places to slide down. They started climbing up to the top.

When Nah-dos-te complained about how heavy her end of the toboggan was, Goyahkla took it away from her and started carrying it by himself.

"Little brother is getting stronger," Ishton teased him.

Goyahkla felt himself blushing. But Ishton was right, he knew. His whole body was changing. He really was getting stronger. Could this be what Alchise was talking about? he wondered.

Finally, they reached the top of the mesa.

"We will slide down here," Nah-dos-te said. She pointed to the steep, gravelly side of the mesa. "It will be the fastest."

"It will also make the most noise," Goyahkla said. Apaches were taught how to hunt and fight without making noise. But when he wasn't doing either of these things, Goyahkla loved to make as much noise as possible.

Nah-dos-te placed the edge of the toboggan at the top of the slide. She and Ishton started to get into the front. But Goyahkla stopped them. "I want to ride in front this time," he said. Before, he had always ridden behind his two sisters. Today, something made him want to change that.

Nah-dos-te and Ishton looked at each other.

Ishton shrugged. "*Little* Brother is beginning to act more like *Big* Brother," she said. But she stepped aside and let Goyahkla take his place in the front beside Nah-dos-te.

Goyahkla watched Nah-dos-te put her feet into the buckskin loops. Then he did the same. Ishton climbed onto the toboggan behind them and put her arms around both their waists.

Suddenly, Goyahkla felt his heart beating fast. He didn't realize how scary it would be sitting in front. Unlike before, there was now no one to keep him from falling out.

"Ready?" Nah-dos-te called.

"Ready!" Ishton said.

But nothing would come from Goyahkla's throat. It felt so dry. He knew his sisters were looking at him. Quickly, he prayed to Usen to give him courage. All of a sudden, he felt his throat relax and he could swallow.

"I think Goyahkla is scared," Nah-dos-te said.

Goyahkla looked at his sister in a way he had never looked before.

Nah-dos-te gasped.

"I am not afraid of anything," Goyahkla shouted to her. With that, he pushed with his right foot and the toboggan started down the side of the mesa.

Nah-dos-te and Ishton were screaming, but Goyahkla knew it was because they were having fun. But he wasn't enjoying the ride at all. He was very angry. He knew he wasn't really angry with Nah-dos-te. She had told the truth. He was angry at himself. He had been afraid. As the wind raced through his hair, he vowed that he would never be afraid again.

When they finally reached the bottom of the mesa, Goyahkla helped Nah-dos-te and Ishton out of the toboggan, then he picked it up, and they all started toward home.

Goyahkla purposely walked faster than his

sisters. He didn't want to talk to them now. He wanted to think.

By the time they got back to their village, Goyahkla had made a decision. He would talk to his father. His father would tell him what things Goyahkla needed to do to become a man.

That evening, Taklishim and Goyahkla went for a moonlit walk on the banks of the Gila River. To Goyahkla, the stars above them had never seemed so bright.

"Your body is changing, Goyahkla. Soon you will no longer be a child," Taklishim said. "Soon you will be taught what you need to know to become an Apache warrior. When the time comes, you must learn your lessons well."

Goyahkla wanted to ask his father exactly how long it would be before he started his lessons, but he knew it was not the Apache way to hurry what had been decided by Usen.

As they continued to walk, Taklishim told Goyahkla of the many tests of endurance he would have to pass. Some of them excited him. Some of them scared him. Goyahkla just hoped that he would not disappoint his family or the rest of the village.

Making Bows and Arrows

Early one morning, when Goyahkla was ten, Kaywaykla, his grandfather on his mother's side, came to the family's tepee. "Greetings, Daughter," Kaywaykla said to Juana. "I have come to teach Goyahkla the ways of the Apache."

Goyahkla jumped up from the antelope blanket he had been sitting on. "I am ready, Grandfather!" he cried. Goyahkla had been waiting for this day to come. Although Taklishim always answered Goyahkla's questions, Apache boys were usually taught the things they needed to know to become great warriors by their grandfathers. Since Goyahkla's other grandfather, the great Chief Mahko, was dead, only Kaywaykla could do that now.

Goyahkla followed Kaywaykla out of the tepee. They headed toward the banks of the Gila River. When they reached the river, Goyahkla spread a large antelope blanket underneath a huge tree. This tree was very special to Goyahkla. Ishton had often told him how, when he was just a few weeks old, it was under this tree that she had rolled him in the dirt in the four directions of the compass.

"Sit with me, Goyahkla, and we will talk of the Apache ways," Kaywaykla began. "The lessons will be long and hard, but if you learn them well, you will become an Apache warrior and will be allowed to take your place beside the other warriors of the village."

Goyahkla wanted to say he thought that he

46

already knew enough, but he kept quiet because he knew to speak such words would not show respect for his elders. But he didn't think he could wait too many more years to be accepted as a man. Maybe, he decided, if he learned quickly, he would impress his father and then Taklishim would let him go on the hunts earlier. That would be his goal—to go on the next hunt with the men of the village.

As they sat together underneath the big tree, Kaywaykla talked to Goyahkla about the rules of hunting.

"We will talk about hunting deer, antelope, elk, mountain lions, and buffalo," Kaywaykla began. "But we will start with the deer, as it is the most important for us to kill."

Goyahkla was glad his grandfather began with talk about killing deer. The deer was prized by the Apaches.

"You must not eat for several days before you hunt deer," Kaywaykla said. "If you are hungry, you will be more successful.

"You must not eat onions," Kaywaykla continued. "You must not wash yourself or wear anything that the deer can smell.

"You must be reverent. You must pray to Usen before the kill. You must be generous with those whose arrows do not find their way to the deer. You must always share part of your kill."

Goyahkla listened closely as his grandfather continued to instruct him in how the Apaches hunted. He told Goyahkla how to make and use a deer-head mask to stalk deer.

"After each hunt we keep a head from one of the deer. Before the next hunt we fill the head with grass so it will once again look like a deer. The deer head is placed on top of a hunter's head."

Goyahkla saw himself on the hunt, a deer head sitting atop his own head.

"The hunter's body is covered with deer hide. Sometimes, the hunter pretends he is grazing, just like the deer do," Kaywaykla continued. "If the hunter is on the open prairie, he has to crawl for several miles in the grass."

"Grandfather, will you show me how to make a leaf whistle to call the deer?" Goyahkla asked.

Kaywaykla nodded. "Take a leaf from the tree," he instructed.

Goyahkla stood up. He chose a leaf from the highest branch he could reach. He handed it to Kaywaykla. Kaywaykla held the leaf horizontally along his lips and blew.

Goyahkla's heart was thrilled. It was a sound he had heard the hunters practice before. "Let me try, Grandfather," he said.

Kaywaykla handed Goyahkla the leaf. Goyahkla held it against his lips and blew. Nothing happened. Goyahkla moved the leaf slightly lower. This time, it made a really funny noise.

Kaywaykla laughed. For a minute, Goyahkla felt embarrassed. But when he tried a third time, he sounded just like the deer hunters!

"It takes practice," Kaywaykla told him. "You will be a good deer caller."

Goyahkla smiled at his grandfather.

Kaywaykla finished the lesson by explaining to Goyahkla how to skin the animal and to cut it up immediately. Then Kaywaykla talked to Goyahkla about how to hunt other animals that the Apache ate. "But to kill animals, you must have a weapon," Kaywaykla said. "I will show you how to make your bow and arrows."

He stood up, stretched, and started back up the trail to the village. Goyahkla followed him. When they finally reached Kaywaykla's tepee, they found Goyahkla's grandmother, Tah-dos-te, sitting outside the opening. She was shucking ears of corn.

"Good morning, Grandmother," Goyahkla greeted her.

"Good morning, Son," Tah-dos-te said.

If Kaywaykla's instruction ended before his

grandmother finished shucking the corn, he would join her, Goyahkla decided. He loved to sit with his grandmother and listen to her tell stories of when she was a child.

Goyahkla followed Kaywaykla inside the tepee. They sat down on an antelope blanket in front of a small fire.

Beside Kaywaykla there was a curved piece of wood. "Last spring, I had you choose a branch from the oak tree we were sitting under today," he said to Goyahkla. "I know it is a special tree in your life."

Goyahkla nodded. "You helped me split it and carve it down," he said. "Then you told me to scrape it smooth with a sharp rock."

Kaywaykla nodded again. "I tied the ends together to give it a curved shape and hung it up in the tepee to season and dry." He handed the curved piece of wood to Goyahkla. But something was wrong.

"It is too stiff, Grandfather," Goyahkla said. "It will not move."

"We are not finished," Kaywaykla replied. He handed Goyahkla a small straw basket that was filled with deer fat. "You must rub this back and forth on the bow to make it bend," he added.

Goyahkla took a handful of the fat. He didn't like the way it felt or smelled. But he wiped it on the curved piece of wood and started rubbing it back and forth. Slowly, the wood of the bow absorbed the fat. Slowly, too, the wood begin to bend in Goyahkla's hand. Finally, Goyahkla thought this piece of wood might actually work for his bow.

"Now we need to make the wood hard," Kaywaykla said. He showed Goyahkla how to rub the bow in the hot ashes of the fire.

When Kaywaykla thought the bow had been hardened enough, Goyahkla took the bow out of the fire. He picked up a handful of sand and used it to wipe off the excess ash. "I want to draw a deer on it, Grandfather," Goyahkla said. "It will bring me good luck when I hunt."

Kaywaykla handed Goyahkla a small straw basket of red paint that had been made from mahogany roots. Using a piece of bone, Goyahkla carefully drew his deer in the center of his bow. When he finished, he was quite proud. Although he would never tell anyone this, he thought it was the best design on any bow in the village, including his father's. He hoped it would bring him good luck in hunting.

When the design had dried, Kaywaykla helped Goyahkla put on the bowstring. They took two sinew strips and rolled them together. They tied them to each end of the bow.

"Are you too tired to help me with the arrows?" Goyahkla asked expectantly.

Kaywaykla shook his head. "I know just where we can find the right branches," he said.

Together, they stood up and left the tepee. Juana, Ishton, and Nah-dos-te had now joined his grandmother to shuck corn. They were giggling about something when Goyahkla and his grandfather came outside.

Goyahkla showed them his bow. Ishton and Nah-dos-te clapped their hands. "It's beautiful, Goyahkla," Ishton said. "You will kill many deer with it. Then I can help Mother make delicious stew."

"You will bring home many skins so I can make myself many beautiful dresses to wear," Nah-dos-te teased him.

Goyahkla smiled at them. He was pleased they were already talking about what a great hunter he would make.

"Goyahkla, I wouldn't mind if you brought home a rabbit tonight," his mother said. "A rabbit stew would taste good, too."

"I don't have any arrows yet, Mother. But Grandfather and I are going to make them now," Goyahkla said. "When I have my arrows, then I will bring home a lot of rabbits."

Kaywaykla grunted.

Goyahkla quickly bowed his head. He

knew he should not be bragging about his hunting skills. This was not the Apache way.

Goyahkla and his grandfather spent the rest of the afternoon and most of the next day making arrows. They cut several small branches from a tree about a mile from the village. Then they peeled off the bark and let the branches dry in the sun. With a sharp stone, Goyahkla made the points of the arrows. Then Kaywaykla showed him how to heat the branches and straighten them with a stone.

Goyahkla knew that in years to come he would make better arrows. He would use mulberry or mahogany, the woods the great warriors used.

But for now, he was quite happy. He finally had his own bow and arrows and he could go hunting, even if he only went hunting for rabbits near the village. Tomorrow, for sure, he decided, he would bring home a rabbit for his mother so she could make her delicious rabbit stew.

56

Hunting with Alchise

One winter morning, very early, before the sun had appeared over the mesa to the east, Goyahkla's grandfather came quietly into the family's tepee.

He knelt beside the sleeping Goyahkla and shook his shoulder. Goyahkla opened his eyes and sat up. His heart was beating fast. He had never before been awakened like this. But he didn't cry out. Apaches learned early that sudden noises in the dark could be dangerous.

By the moonlight streaming into the top of

the tepee, Goyahkla could just make out the outline of his grandfather. Goyahkla shivered. "What is it, Grandfather?" he whispered.

"Come with me," Kaywaykla whispered back.

Goyahkla dressed hurriedly, then followed Kaywaykla out of the tepee. Moonlight glistened off a light snow that had fallen during the night. Goyahkla and his grandfather left the village and headed toward the Gila River. When they reached the banks, Kaywaykla said, "Find sticks. We must build a fire."

Now the moon was hidden behind snow clouds, so Goyahkla picked up what sticks he could see. When he thought he had enough, he put them together in the shape of a tepee and placed dried leaves in the center. He was prepared to use two rocks, hitting them together to cause sparks, to start the fire, but his grandfather handed him a burning ember that he had carried in a special pouch.

Goyahkla placed the ember on top of the

bed of leaves, and shortly a blazing fire began to crackle.

"You have had your twelfth birthday, Goyahkla," Kaywaykla said. "It is now time for the ceremonial bathing in the river."

Goyahkla shivered just thinking about how the cold water would feel against his skin, but he knew that this was part of his passage into manhood. Bathing like this cleansed the spirit and hardened the body.

Goyahkla took off his clothes and stood naked before the fire. Kaywaykla first prayed to Usen, then Goyahkla headed toward the banks of the Gila River.

Apache boys and girls were very good swimmers. During the summers, Goyahkla enjoyed swimming in the river. It was the best way to cool off when the days got really hot. But this morning, he knew, the water would only make him feel colder.

His foot first touched not water but a thin layer of ice. As his foot plunged through the ice, Goyahkla felt a numbing sensation. He wondered if he would freeze and not be able to get out of the river. If that happened, he would embarrass his whole family. He took a deep breath and jumped into the river, falling below the surface. He jumped up and down, willing his body to believe it was still summer and that he and his friends were playing in the river. Now his whole body felt numb. Quickly, Goyahkla turned around and headed back toward the bank.

As he stepped out, the winds seem to freeze the water that clung to his skin. He could see his grandfather standing next to the fire. Goyahkla wanted to run toward its warmth, but no Apache warrior would do that. He willed himself to walk at a measured pace back to the fire. Finally, he reached the fire.

Goyahkla rubbed his hands over the flames and slowly turned around and around. The heat began to bring feeling back to his body. In a few minutes, all the numbness was gone.

Kaywaykla put a hand on Goyahkla's shoulder. "It is time for you to return to the river," he said.

Goyahkla turned and started back toward the river. But now it wasn't so bad, because he knew that no matter how frozen his body felt, the warm fire would bring it back to normal.

When Goyahkla reached the river, he again plunged into its freezing water. He jumped up and down, ceremonially cleansing his body and his spirit. Then he went back to the fire to warm himself.

After Goyahkla had done this four times, Kaywaykla said, "It is time to return to the village. Your mother has prepared a special meal for you."

At the thought of warm food, Goyahkla's stomach started to grumble. He dressed hurriedly.

"I knew that would make you happy," Kaywaykla said.

Goyahkla grinned. "Yes, Grandfather, swimming always makes me hungry."

Just as Goyahkla and his family were finishing breakfast, Alchise came by their tepee. "Come, Goyahkla! Four boys from the village on the other side of the mountain are here!" he said excitedly. "They want us to go hunting with them! It's a contest!"

Goyahkla grabbed his bow and arrows and followed Alchise to the center of the village, where the boys were waiting for them.

The four boys nodded their greetings to Goyahkla. Goyahkla nodded back.

Goyahkla believed he had become a very good hunter over the last two years. Sometimes he hunted with Alchise. Sometimes he hunted by himself. Often, when he was in the woods or on the prairie, he met up with boys from nearby Apache villages, and they were always impressed by how many rabbits and other small game he had bagged.

Of course, Goyahkla was sure that Usen would be angry with him for being so pleased with himself, but he had heard that boys from neighboring villages invited only the best hunters from other villages to go with them. So if these four boys wanted him and Alchise to go hunting with them now, Goyahkla thought they were probably getting close to the time when they would be asked to accompany the warriors of their own village on a great hunting expedition.

"You and I will hunt side by side," Alchise said. "When we all return to the village, we will divide the game and distribute it evenly between our two villages."

Goyahkla nodded. "That is a good idea," he said. He was impressed by Alchise. Alchise was already sounding like an Apache chief. Goyahkla knew that Apache chiefs were chosen because they were great warriors and could take care of the people in the village. They were not chosen because they were the sons of other chiefs. Even though Goyahkla's father's father had been the great Chief Mahko, that didn't mean his son or Goyahkla would be chief.

The boys started out of the village. Goyahkla and Alchise headed toward the mesas where Goyahkla had enjoyed sliding down the slopes in the toboggan that Alchise had built. He started to tell Alchise how much fun it had been, but decided he needed to keep his mind on the hunt.

"I have seen prairie chickens on the other side of the mesas," Alchise said. "They make delicious stews."

Goyahkla's mouth began to water as he thought about all the prairie chickens he and Alchise would shoot, and once again he had to remind himself that Usen did not like Apaches to be too confident. If they were, then Usen would often make the game scarce so they would return from the hunt without anything. Silently, Goyahkla prayed to Usen to clear his mind of pride.

Goyahkla and Alchise skirted around the two mesas and continued their way eastward. When they were about two miles from the mesas, Alchise stopped.

Instantly, Goyahkla stopped, too. They stood as still as the trunk of a tree.

"See that clump of bushes straight ahead?" Alchise whispered.

Goyahkla nodded.

"I think there is a flock of prairie chickens on the other side," Alchise added.

Goyahkla strained to see if he could detect any movement through the leaves and branches of the bushes. Finally, he thought he could tell the difference between the color of the branches and the color of the feathers of the prairie chickens.

"Yes, Alchise, they are there."

Alchise and Goyahkla silently got down on their stomachs and began crawling toward the bushes. They had been trained to creep up on animals and enemies this way.

Slowly, Alchise and Goyahkla made their way to the bush. All of a sudden, two of the prairie chickens came around to the front of the bush. Alchise and Goyahkla stopped crawling.

"I think we're close enough to hit them from here," Alchise whispered.

Alchise retrieved an arrow from his quiver. Goyahkla did the same. Carefully, they both rose to a crouched position.

"I'll take the one on the left," Alchise whispered. "You take the one on the right."

"All right," Goyahkla whispered back.

Goyahkla got the arrow ready and pulled back on the bow.

"Ready?" Alchise whispered.

"Ready," Goyahkla whispered back.

They released their arrows at the same time. Goyahkla watched as the arrows flew through the air, barely two feet above the ground, toward the prairie chickens.

The arrows found their marks. The two

prairie chickens flopped to the ground with barely a sound. But it was enough to make three other chickens come around to see what had happened.

Quickly, Alchise and Goyahkla readied two more arrows. These arrows found their marks as well, and now four prairie chickens were lying on the ground.

The remaining prairie chicken seemed unsure what to do, now that the other four weren't moving, but it started running away from the bush. Alchise and Goyahkla were on their feet after it.

"It's yours!" Alchise shouted.

Goyahkla readied an arrow. The first one missed, but Goyahkla continued to chase the prairie chicken. The second arrow missed, too. But Goyahkla aimed a third arrow at the prairie chicken, and this time it found its mark. The prairie chicken flopped to the ground. Goyahkla picked it up proudly and held it above his head.

Alchise clapped his approval. Then he helped Goyahkla locate the two stray arrows.

They gathered up the rest of the prairie chickens and headed back to the village, their arms around each other's shoulders.

"Tonight, after we eat, we can challenge the boys from the village on the other side of the mountain to a game of hide-and-seek," Alchise said. "They won't know our best hiding places, like the boys in our village do."

"That's a good idea," Goyahkla said.

He enjoyed playing hide-and-seek. It was fun. But it was also a valuable game. It was important for a warrior to know how to conceal himself so he could ambush an enemy.

When Goyahkla and Alchise got back to their village, the other boys were waiting for them in front of Goyahkla's tepee. They had shot only a few rabbits and a couple of squirrels but, even though they had lost the contest, they were delighted to see the prairie chickens that Alchise and Goyahkla had bagged.

"I love prairie chicken stew," one of the boys said. "We don't get to eat it very much, though. There aren't many prairie chickens near our village."

"We can fix that," Juana said to them.

While the boys all sat around, resting and telling stories about their different hunting trips, Juana, Ishton, and Nah-dos-te cleaned the prairie chickens.

Juana used three of them to make a big pot of stew. She put the two remaining prairie chickens in a small basket so the boys could take them back to their village.

Ishton put all of the feathers in a small basket. Later, she would use them for decorations.

The boys kept telling Juana how wonderful the prairie chicken stew was, and she kept giving them refills.

Finally, the stew was all gone, and the game of hide-and-seek began.

Each time Goyahkla and Alchise hid, the four boys could never find them. Each time the four boys hid, Goyahkla and Alchise found them after only a few minutes.

Finally, the boys had had enough. "You're too clever for us," they said. "Show us how to hide so we can't be found."

So Goyahkla and Alchise told them their secrets. They showed the four boys how to blend in with the trees and the bushes. They showed them how to slither across the ground so no one would see them coming.

It worked. When they played one last game, it took Goyahkla and Alchise much longer to find them.

By the time the four boys left the Bedonkohe village, it was very late, but they assured everyone that they could find their way back to their village with their eyes closed.

Goyahkla and Alchise watched the four boys disappear into the darkness. Even though they lived in a village on the other side of the mountain, they were still Apaches, Goyahkla knew, and all Apaches were brothers. They all shared their knowledge with one another so that the entire Apache nation would continue to survive.

Running up the Mountain

As the winter turned into spring, Goyahkla began to grow restless. He wanted to hunt with the men of the village. In his heart he knew he could hunt as well as any of them. He wanted to join them in battle, too.

But Goyahkla wasn't the only one in his village who was restless. So were many of the warriors. For as long as Goyahkla could remember, there had been peace, but the Mexicans to the south were beginning to come onto Apache lands more and more frequently. Goyahkla's father said the Mexicans were beginning to talk as if Apache lands were their lands.

Goyahkla had also begun to hear talk about Americans, a strange new people whom the Apaches called "white eyes." They were coming onto Apache lands from the east. Though the Apaches didn't mind sharing their land, the idea of anyone *owning* the land was inconceivable to them. But the Mexicans and the Americans were starting to make the Apaches feel as if they weren't supposed to be there at all.

Goyahkla finally got up the nerve to tell his grandfather how he felt. "You still have much to learn before you can sit at the fires with the rest of the men, Goyahkla," Kaywaykla said. "Your body must be your only friend."

"What do you mean, Grandfather?" Goyahkla asked.

"When you are a man, Goyahkla, no one can help you but yourself," Kaywaykla replied. "Your only true friends will be your

74

legs, your eyes, your ears, your arms, your hands, and your head."

Goyahkla had never thought about this before. Alchise was his best friend. But did this mean that Alchise might not help him if he needed it?

"You must teach your legs to run faster than a deer. You must teach your eyes to see like an eagle," Kaywaykla continued. "You must teach your ears to hear what you cannot see at night when there is no moon. You must teach your arms and hands to be strong and quick like the mountain lion. You must teach your head to guide you to do the right thing."

"If I do all these things, Grandfather, will I be a great Apache warrior?" Goyahkla asked.

Kaywaykla nodded. "Then I will teach my body to do these things," Goyahkla said. "May I begin now?"

Kaywaykla smiled. "Yes, Grandson," he replied.

Alchise had told him several months

before what the first test would be. Goyahkla would have to fill his mouth with water and then run to the top of a mountain and back without swallowing or spitting the water out. When Goyahkla asked Alchise why he had to do this, Alchise told him that it trained Apache warriors to breathe through their noses. If they knew how to breathe right, they would never get tired.

After Alchise told him about this test, Goyahkla got up early every morning. He filled his mouth with water and practiced breathing through his nose. Goyahkla practiced doing this almost every day so he would not fail the test.

But now he was nervous. What if he did swallow the water? He would never become an Apache warrior if he did that.

Goyahkla stood up. Just as he finished taking off all of his clothes except for a buckskin loincloth, he felt the presence of somebody behind him. He turned. It was Gil-tee, a boy from one of the neighboring villages. What was he doing here? Goyahkla wondered.

Almost as if he could read Goyahkla's thoughts, his grandfather said, "Gil-tee will follow you to the top of the mountain."

Goyahkla knew Gil-tee very well. He had hunted with him before. He didn't like him. He didn't trust him. Gil-tee never divided his game fairly. Goyahkla wanted to tell his grandfather that he would like to have somebody else go with him to the top of the mountain, but he knew he couldn't say anything like that. That would be disrespectful. Goyahkla could only hope that Gil-tee would tell the truth about him. But what if Gil-tee told the other warriors in the village that Goyahkla swallowed his water and put some more in his mouth from the Gila River? Would the warriors believe Gil-tee?

Gil-tee grinned at Goyahkla. He picked up the water jug and handed it to him. Goyahkla put the jug to his lips and took a mouthful of water.

"Go!" Kaywaykla shouted.

Goyahkla and Gil-tee started out of the village. Goyahkla noticed that several people in the village were watching them. He decided to keep his eyes straight ahead and not think about what would happen if he swallowed the water.

He and Gil-tee headed out of the village and down the path toward the Gila River. When they reached the banks, Gil-tee jumped in and started swimming. Goyahkla did the same, but some water from the river went up one of his nostrils, almost choking him. He hurriedly breathed out his nose several times, expelling most of the river water, but not losing the water in his mouth.

Don't think about it! Don't think about it! he kept telling himself. By the time he was in the middle of the river, his mind had convinced his throat that it didn't need to cough.

Gil-tee reached the other side and stood on the banks, hands on his hips, grinning at Goyahkla.

78

He wants me to fail this test, Goyahkla thought. He doesn't think I can do it.

Anger surged through Goyahkla. But he quickly asked Usen for forgiveness and started up the mountain, pushing his body as hard as he could. Gil-tee was startled by Goyahkla's sudden burst of speed and had to race to catch up with him.

Goyahkla jumped huge boulders and dodged mesquite bushes and cactus. But Gil-tee was right behind him. Gil-tee didn't seem to be having any problems at all with the climb. But Goyahkla knew the steepest part of the mountain was ahead of them. He prayed again to Usen that his legs would find sure footing.

Suddenly, behind him, he heard Gil-tee yell. Goyahkla stopped and looked back. He would never forget what he saw: A huge rattlesnake was hanging by its fangs from Gil-tee's legs.

Goyahkla unsheathed his knife and started back down toward Gil-tee.

"No!" Gil-tee screamed. With one hand he had grasped the head of the rattlesnake and was pulling the fangs out of his leg. "You must go on up the mountain," he called to Goyahkla.

Goyahkla shook his head. He couldn't leave Gil-tee like this.

"I can take care of myself," Gil-tee called to him. With his other hand, Gil-tee had now unsheathed his knife. With a flashing motion he cut off the head of the rattlesnake and threw its body into a nearby mesquite tree.

Goyahkla took a few more steps down the mountain toward Gil-tee.

Now Gil-tee had cut his leg where the snake had bitten him and was sucking out the blood. He spit out his blood and screamed, "If you don't go up the mountain, I will tell the warriors of your village that you swallowed your water."

He really doesn't want me to help him, Goyahkla realized. He thinks it's a sign of weakness. Now he understood what his grandfather had told him: "Your body must be your only friend. . . . No one can help you but yourself." Gil-tee understood that. He knew how to survive even if bitten by a rattlesnake.

Goyahkla raised his hand in a salute. With a weak smile, Gil-tee returned it.

With that, Goyahkla turned and headed back up the mountain.

In just a few minutes the steep part of the run started, and sweat began to pour off Goyahkla. Every muscle in his body felt as though it were being pulled in all directions. Now his throat burned from his breathing only through his nostrils.

He dodged more boulders, almost slipping several times because of loose rocks, but he finally reached the top.

He stood for a minute and looked down at the village. He wondered if anybody was looking up at him. Then he prayed to Usen, asking forgiveness for being so conceited. Now his eyes found Gil-tee. He was standing. Goyahkla hoped he would be all right.

He started back down the mountain. Going down would be easier, he knew, but he would have to be careful not to stumble. He wanted to run into the village. He didn't want to tumble into it.

When he reached Gil-tee, he started to slow down, but Gil-tee fell into the same pace as Goyahkla.

Goyahkla could see in Gil-tee's eyes that he was in pain, but Gil-tee said nothing. That was the Apache way.

Finally they reached the Gila River and swam across. There were some young boys waiting for them on the bank. They followed Goyahkla and Gil-tee into the village, where Kaywaykla and several other warriors and braves were gathered together.

Warriors were the most important Apache men. They fought in all of the battles and went on all of the major hunts. They were the only ones allowed to wear the war cap adorned with turkey and eagle feathers.

Braves were older boys who were still going through the rituals on the way to becoming warriors. From time to time warriors would ask some of the braves to accompany them in battle or on hunts. That was a sign to the braves that the warriors of the village thought they were worthy of being warriors.

"Goyahkla went to the top of the mountain," Gil-tee reported. "He still has the water from the jug in his mouth." At that, Goyahkla spit out the water.

The villagers clapped their hands.

Goyahkla could see in everyone's eyes that the warriors and braves were beginning to think of him as a man.

Gil-tee held out his hand to Goyahkla. "Brother, go with me to Teo's tepee. He has strong medicine for snakebites," he said. "We can also talk about all the battles we're going to fight together."

Goyahkla smiled and took Gil-tee's arm. Together, they headed toward the medicine man's tepee on the banks of the river.

The First Buffalo Hunt

One morning, shortly after the water challenge, some of the braves in the village decided to have a contest to see who could shoot an arrow the farthest. They asked Goyahkla and Alchise to join them. Several of the younger warriors came to watch.

Goyahkla and Alchise gave each other quick, knowing grins. An invitation to such a contest meant that the warriors of the village now believed Goyahkla and Alchise were far enough along in their coming-of-age rituals for them to be considered braves, too.

Goyahkla was the first to shoot. He pulled his best arrow out of the quiver and aimed. He pulled the bowstring back as far as he could and let it go. The arrow went higher and farther than he had ever shot one before.

Goyahkla felt like jumping up and down and shouting, but he knew that braves did not do such things. Still, he couldn't help being proud. He hoped that Usen wouldn't be angry with him.

He could tell from the looks on the warriors' faces that they were impressed.

When all the other braves had finished, it was Goyahkla's arrow that had gone the farthest. Several of the warriors slapped him on the back and congratulated him.

"You will kill many buffalo if you always shoot like that," Nautzile told him.

"You will kill many deer and antelope, too," Kadinschin said.

Cadete, another one of the warriors, stepped up and gave Goyahkla a hard look.

"You will also kill many Mexicans and white eyes," he said.

Goyahkla blinked. He had long wanted to go into battle, but this was the first time he had ever thought about *killing* anything except animals to eat.

"We are at peace now, Cadete," Kadinschin said. "We will not talk of killing men."

Cadete's nostrils flared. He turned to Kadinschin. "But there will soon be war, Kadinschin! The Mexicans and the Americans are taking over our lands," he said. "Goyahkla and the rest of the braves need to think about killing these invaders instead of always thinking about killing game." With that, Cadete stalked off.

For several minutes, no one said anything, then Nautzile turned to the braves and said, "We warriors challenge you to a footrace!"

The braves cheered.

Goyahkla knew that the braves who won these contests were always the first to be invited to go on a large game hunt with the warriors.

Several other warriors had now joined the group.

"We will race barefoot to the largest of the two mesas and back," Nautzile said.

The warriors and the braves took off their moccasins. Goyahkla's feet were already toughened by having played barefoot in the village. He had purposely kept them that way, knowing that one day he would be tested by having to race the warriors without his moccasins.

The warriors and the braves lined up.

Nautzile shouted, "Go!"

The group raced out of the village toward the two mesas. Goyahkla was quickly ahead of the other braves but behind most of the warriors. Only Alchise was close to him.

Goyahkla remembered what he had learned on the race up the mountain with his mouth full of water. He kept his mouth tightly closed and breathed through his nose.

Slowly, he gained on several of the warriors and was soon ahead of them.

When he reached the big mesa he touched the base, and then headed back toward the village. He passed even more of the warriors.

Goyahkla pushed his legs harder. Silently, he prayed to Usen. He wanted to show the warriors how strong he was. He wanted to show them that he was ready to go with them.

Finally, Goyahkla reached the starting point. He touched Nautzile's hand.

Several minutes later the last of the braves trotted into the village. The warriors gathered everyone together.

"Tomorrow morning we leave on a buffalo hunt. We will be gone for several days," Kadinschin announced. "If Usen wills it, we will return with much meat and many warm hides. Since Goyahkla and Alchise have proven themselves in smaller hunts around the village, they will now accompany us."

The braves all cheered and started slapping Goyahkla and Alchise on their backs and congratulating them.

Goyahkla's father walked up to him and put his hands on Goyahkla's shoulders. "I am proud of you," he said. "If your grandfather, the great Chief Mahko, were here, he would be proud of you, too."

"Thank you, Father," Goyahkla said. His heart was so swollen with pride, he could hardly say anything else. All of his life he had looked forward to this moment. "I will not disappoint you," Goyahkla added.

Goyahkla could hardly sleep that night. He tossed and turned underneath his antelope blanket. At dawn, he heard his father stirring. He threw back the covers and dressed quickly.

By the time his mother and sisters were up, he was standing by the door to the tepee, waiting for his father.

"Goyahkla!" his father called from inside. "You have forgotten to eat breakfast."

Goyahkla felt silly. He knew he would have

to have a full stomach if he planned to keep his mind on the hunt. He quickly went inside.

Everyone was grinning at him. Only momentarily angry, Goyahkla grinned back.

"It is all right, my son," his father said. "I remember the first time I went with the warriors. It is an important event in our lives."

"Thank you for telling me that, Father," Goyahkla said. He wanted his father to be proud of him. He didn't want to do foolish boy things anymore.

His mother's delicious rabbit stew warmed the insides of his stomach. He was even allowed a third helping. Finally, it was time to leave.

Taklishim and Goyahkla left the tepee together and headed toward the corral where the ponies were kept. Goyahkla saw some of the younger boys holding the ponies for the warriors. Goyahkla remembered when he used to do this and would dream of going with the warriors on a big game hunt. Now the time had come.

"Here, Goyahkla!" a voice called to him. Goyahkla turned. Skinya, one of the smallest boys in the village, was holding the reins of a beautiful mustang. "This is the horse your father chose for you. I put the rope on him myself."

Goyahkla hurried over and clapped Skinya on the back. "Thank you," he said. "I will bring you back something special from the hunt."

"Usen willing," Skinya said.

"Usen willing," Goyahkla agreed. He knew that he should be more humble, but the excitement of what was happening was beginning to overtake him.

Goyahkla rode alongside his father. They were in the middle of the large group of warriors. Alchise was riding beside his father, several horses behind Goyahkla. From time to time, though, they would grin at each other. Goyahkla thought he knew what Alchise was thinking: Once they found the buffalo, they would prove their right to be here.

After almost a day of riding, the Apaches arrived at a valley that would allow them to reach flatter land, where the buffalo would be, instead of riding over the mountains. There they spent the first night. Goyahkla was so tired that even the excitement of what was to come couldn't keep him awake. When his father shook his shoulder the next morning, he was sure that he had just lain down.

After a cold breakfast of deer meat, they were on their way again.

It took two more days before they actually reached the herds of buffalo. Along the way, they had seen people from other tribes. Taklishim told Goyahkla they were called Comanche and Kiowa. They lived on the flat plains, he explained. They didn't stop the Apache from hunting the buffalo, but Taklishim added that the Comanches and the Kiowas were not friends of the Apaches.

Goyahkla was amazed when he first saw the buffalo herd. They seemed to stretch from horizon to horizon. No wonder the Comanches and the Kiowas let us hunt them in peace, he thought. There is no way they could ever eat them all.

"We will camp here tonight," Kadinschin announced. "We will kill the buffalo tomorrow."

For the next few days, the Apaches chased the buffalo on their ponies. They rode close and killed them with arrows and spears.

Goyahkla and Alchise rode together.

"I'll head this one off," Goyahkla called to Alchise. He rode toward a big bull that seemed to be going in all directions. The bull's horns just missed the flank of his pony. Goyahkla breathed a sigh of relief. If his pony was hurt, Goyahkla would have to destroy him and he would have to walk back to the village. His father and the other warriors would think that he still had much to learn before he could go on another big game hunt. It was important that a warrior take care of his horse. His horse was his other legs.

Goyahkla circled this big bull again. This time, he made sure that his pony was not in harm's way. Suddenly, the bull stopped. So did Goyahkla. Goyahkla knew that the bull was planning to charge him. But just as the bull snorted, Alchise came up from behind and plunged a spear into his stomach.

The big bull collapsed onto the ground.

Goyahkla and Alchise let out loud whoops. They had killed their first buffalo.

By the end of the hunt, Goyahkla and Alchise and the rest of the Apache band had each killed about three buffalo. They skinned them and butchered them on the spot, then loaded their ponies with the skins and the meat.

As they headed back toward their village, Goyahkla wondered what he would see in the eyes of his mother and his sisters and the other girls in the village. He was sure they would be thinking that now Goyahkla was equal to the warriors in the village.

Juh

In the weeks and months that followed, when the warriors went hunting for deer or buffalo, they asked Goyahkla and Alchise to go with them.

Then one morning, Cadete called Goyahkla and Alchise to his tepee. "There are some cougars in the mountains. They have killed our brothers' children in the village in the next valley," he said. "Our brothers have asked us to help them hunt the cougars."

"We are ready to go," Goyahkla said.

He and Alchise ran to their tepees to get their bows and arrows.

The warriors rode out of the village and headed into the mountains in search of the cougars. They found a lair of them in a cave several miles from their village.

Goyahkla killed several cougars with arrows and one with a spear, then he and Alchise helped tie the cougars to the backs of the horses so they could carry them home.

"We have helped our Apache brothers," Kadinschin said. "We also now have meat for the people of our village."

Goyahkla enjoyed eating cougar meat. They didn't often have it in their village. The big cats usually stayed on the other side of the mountains.

Goyahkla also knew that the hide of the cougars was good for making quivers for their arrows. It had been a very successful hunt.

But Goyahkla didn't spend all of his time hunting. Since the Apaches weren't at war, they had time to grow vegetables in the fertile valley soil near the village. Each family had its own plot of land.

"It is time to plant the fields," Taklishim said one morning at breakfast. "Today we will plant the corn, the beans, and the pumpkins."

Although it was hard work, Goyahkla enjoyed helping his family in the fields. It made him happy to be with his family, for they talked and laughed as they worked together.

There, Goyahkla felt closest to Usen. As Goyahkla broke the ground with a sharp wooden stick his grandfather had made for him, he gave thanks for all the good things that the Apaches had been given.

When the ground was ready, Taklishim and Juana gave Ishton, Nah-dos-te, and Goyahkla the grains and seeds they would need. Goyahkla received the grains of corn. "I will plant the corn in long rows in the way of our ancestors," he said.

He put the first grains of corn in the ground, and then his family helped him plant the rest of the grains.

Ishton received the beans. "I will plant the beans among the corn in the way our ancestors did," she said.

She planted beans in holes on either side of where the corn was planted. When she finished, the rest of the family helped her plant the remaining beans.

Nah-dos-te was given the pumpkin seeds. "I will plant these around the corn and the beans in the way our ancestors did," she said. "The pumpkins and their vines will protect the corn and the beans." She planted several pumpkin seeds in irregular order around some of the corn and beans, then Goyahkla and Ishton helped her plant the rest.

When they finished, Taklishim led them in a prayer to Usen. He asked that Usen give the plants rain when they needed it.

Over the next few months, Goyahkla's

family would go together to their fields to cultivate them. In the early morning and in the late afternoon they would pull the weeds so that only the corn, bean, and pumpkin plants would get the moisture and nourishment from the soil.

One day, when the plants had grown to where they reached Goyahkla's waist, Juana said, "Goyahkla, this evening you and your sisters will walk among the plants to make sure the deer and rabbits do not eat them before they're ready to harvest."

Goyahkla was disappointed. He and Alchise had planned to practice shooting their arrows at targets. But Goyahkla knew how important it was to keep the animals away from their food. If they didn't, there might not be very much to eat when winter came.

That evening, just as the sun was setting, Goyahkla and his sisters joined several of the other boys and girls of the village in the fields. They talked and laughed and made enough noise that most of the animals stayed away.

Goyahkla had even brought along his slingshot, just in case he spotted a brave rabbit. "There's one!" his friend Chinga whispered to him.

Goyahkla looked just in time to see a brown rabbit nibbling at one of their bean plants. "No, you don't!" Goyahkla whispered back. He readied a rock in his slingshot, aimed it at the rabbit, and let go. It hit its mark.

Before it was time to go back to the village, Goyahkla had killed two more rabbits, enough for his mother to make a big pot of rabbit stew.

Because of Goyahkla's marksmanship, his family ate rabbit stew a lot during the summer and into the fall, before the crops were ready to harvest.

Then, one day, after the leaves on the trees began to turn colors and a chill appeared in the air, Taklishim said, "Today, the whole village will harvest what we planted in the spring."

Except for some of the elders, who stayed in the village, the rest of the Apaches walked to the valley to begin the harvest.

Goyahkla, Ishton, and Nah-dos-te helped their parents gather the pumpkins and beans. They put them in baskets that the women elders of the village had woven for this occasion. After they finished with the pumpkins and the beans, the family tied the ears of corn together by the husks.

When all of the crops had been gathered, the harvest was carried to the village on the backs of the ponies. That evening, after supper, everyone helped shuck the corn.

The next morning, Goyahkla went with his father and the other men to caves in the mountains above the village. When Goyahkla and his father had selected their cave, Taklishim said, "Help me carry rocks and tree branches inside to put on the floor."

Goyahkla looked for the flattest rocks and the strongest branches and carried them to the cave. He helped Taklishim arrange them so that they were distributed evenly.

"Now we will put the containers of food on top of the rocks and the branches," Taklishim said. "This will help keep everything safe from the insects that live in the ground."

When they finished storing all the containers of food, Goyahkla said, "I know what to do now, Father. We must seal up the entrance to keep the bears and the cougars and the deer from eating it."

"You are right, Goyahkla," Taklishim said.

Together, they gathered huge rocks. They began stacking them at the entrance to the cave. When the rocks had reached the top, Goyahkla and Taklishim filled in the spaces between the rocks with mud.

"Our food is safe now," Goyahkla said. He stepped back and admired their work. "No animal can eat it before our family does."

The rest of the Apaches had finished with their caves, too, so they started back down the mountain toward the village. When they arrived, Goyahkla saw that they had visitors. "It is the Nednai Apaches from Mexico," Taklishim said to Goyahkla. "Come. Let's welcome them."

But the welcome had already started. There was much hugging and laughing and slapping on the back as family members greeted other family members they hadn't seen for many moons.

As Goyahkla watched, someone shoved him from behind. Angrily, he whirled around.

He was looking into the face of a heavyset boy about his own age. "I-I-I-I'm Juh. My f-f-father is a great c-c-chief," the boy stammered. "I have k-k-k-killed many deer in Mexico."

"I have killed many deer here, too," Goyahkla said.

"If we h-h-have a contest, I w-w-will beat you," Juh challenged him.

Goyahkla had already decided that he didn't like this boy who called himself Juh. But Apache custom forbid him not to be welcoming.

"Maybe," Goyahkla said.

He was spared further dealings with Juh by the arrival of Ishton and some of the Nednai girls. Goyahkla noticed Juh staring at Ishton. Why is he doing that? he wondered.

"We're going into the woods to pick acorns, Goyahkla," Ishton said. She smiled at Juh. "Do you want to come with us?"

"No, not today," Goyahkla said.

He had seen the warriors of his village talking to the Nednai warriors. He was sure they were talking about what the Mexicans were doing on Apache land. If the Apaches had to fight the Mexicans, Goyahkla wanted to know more about them.

"All right," Ishton said. "But when I'm

eating them tonight, don't ask me for some," she teased.

Goyahkla ignored her. He started toward the warriors. He thought Juh would follow him. When he didn't, he shrugged. I have better things to do than waste my time with him, he thought.

The stories the Nednai warriors told thrilled Goyahkla. It almost made him wish that the Apaches were at war with the Mexicans.

But in the middle of one particularly exciting story, he felt someone pull on his shoulder.

He turned. It was his grandmother, the wife of the great Chief Mahko.

"What is it, Grandmother?" Goyahkla asked.

"Your sister, Ishton, and some of the other girls went into the woods to pick acorns," his grandmother said. "When they were finished, that Nednai boy, Juh, and some of his Nednai friends grabbed all their acorns and ran away with them."

Goyahkla felt the anger rising within him.

"What is your wish, Grandmother?" he asked.

"I want you to waylay Juh and his friends and teach them a lesson," his grandmother replied calmly. "I want you to give them a good whipping."

Goyahkla was glad to obey his grandmother's wishes. There was nothing he would like better than to put Juh in his place.

Goyahkla left the group of warriors and hurried into the woods. He found Juh and the other Nednai boys sitting on the ground eating the acorns.

Goyahkla lunged at Juh, pinning him to the earth. The other Nednai boys jumped up and fled. Goyahkla's face was only inches from Juh's. "Is this what Nednai braves do, Juh?" he demanded. "Steal from the girls in the village?"

"No! Nednais are b-b-brave warriors, t-t-too," Juh managed to say. "We w-w-were only j-j-joking with them."

Goyahkla released Juh and allowed him to sit up.

"You stole my sisters' acorns," Goyahkla said. "I promised my grandmother that I would punish you."

"Wh-wh-what do y-y-you plan to d-d-do?" Juh stammered.

Goyahkla thought for several minutes. There was nothing he'd like to do more than give Juh a whipping, but he finally decided that wouldn't solve the problem.

"You're going to fill my sister's basket with more acorns," Goyahkla finally said. "Then you're going to take it to her and apologize."

"Ok-k-kay," Juh said.

For the next hour they searched the woods for the remaining acorns. Several times Juh climbed high into the trees to get the best ones.

As they walked, Juh talked about life in Mexico among the Nednai Apaches. Goyahkla was surprised that he actually enjoyed listening to him. Finally, Ishton's basket was once again full of acorns.

111

Goyahkla and Juh headed back to the village. Goyahkla was no longer angry. Maybe Juh wasn't really so bad after all, he decided. But at that moment, Goyahkla had no idea that one day Juh would marry Ishton and become his brother-in-law.

Fighting a Bear

The seasons came and went in the Bedonkohe village. Goyahkla and Alchise spent almost all of their time with the other braves, preparing themselves for the day when they would take their places alongside the warriors.

One morning, as Goyahkla and his father were getting ready to leave on a buffalo hunt, there were shouts from outside the family's tepee.

"Taklishim! Juana! Come quickly!" several voices called.

Goyahkla's father and mother jumped up

113

from their breakfast and ran out of the tepee. Goyahkla, Ishton, and Nah-dos-te followed them.

Several of the men and women of the village were standing by a pony. The pony had baskets of berries hanging from each side of it.

"It's Nana's horse!" Juana cried. "But where is Nana?"

"The horse came in by itself this morning," Cadete said. "Something bad has happened to Nana."

The women started moaning. Nana was one of the oldest women in the village. But she was still strong, and she loved to go berry picking in the mountains.

"We have to search for her!" one of the women cried.

Nana's family had all been killed by Mexicans a long time ago. Everyone in Goyahkla's village looked after her. She was everyone's grandmother.

114

The men exchanged glances. They knew the woman was right, but they were leaving that morning for a big hunt. The buffalo were heading north, and if they didn't leave today, the buffalo might get too far away. The village needed the meat to survive. The Apaches didn't like to hunt too far into the land of the Comanches.

Goyahkla could tell that his mother and the other women of the village were very upset. He made a decision. "I will not go on the hunt," Goyahkla announced. "I will go look for Nana."

His father clasped his hand. "This is a brave thing that you do, Goyahkla," he said.

Goyahkla embraced his father. Then he watched solemnly as his father and the rest of the warriors and the braves headed out of the village toward the prairies to the northeast.

"I will bring you back an extra thick buffalo hide!" Alchise called to him.

"That is good!" Goyahkla shouted.

When he could no longer see the warriors and the braves, Goyahkla readied his own pony.

"I will pray to Usen that you find Nana and bring her back home safely," Juana told him.

With a wave of his hand, Goyahkla started out of the village toward the high mountains that lay beyond. No one had talked about what might have happened to Nana. But Goyahkla knew that there were many grizzlies and black and brown bears in the mountains.

Several times, over the last few years, bears had come close to where the Apaches had hidden food in caves. Some Apaches would not eat bear meat because bears walked upright like people. These Apaches believed that the spirit of their wicked ancestors sometimes returned to earth in the body of a bear. But not all Apaches felt this way. The people in Goyahkla's village thought that bear meat was good. They also valued the skin of the bear, and used bear grease for oiling guns and for greasing women's hair.

Most Apaches would not go out of their way to hunt bears. In fact, they tried to avoid them. But no Apache would refuse to fight a bear if there was a good reason. As Goyahkla headed up into the mountains, he thought that if a bear had harmed Nana, he would kill the bear and bring it back down to the village.

Slowly, Goyahkla's pony climbed higher and higher up the side of the mountain. Goyahkla liked the smell of the pine trees. It was different from the smell of the earth of his village. But the undergrowth was so thick that it made travel difficult.

When Goyahkla reached the place where he knew Nana liked to look for berries, he dismounted. Some branches were broken on one of the bushes. Someone had gone through this way recently. He tied his horse to a strong branch and started through the undergrowth.

A loud growl came from somewhere in the woods. It was followed by a scream.

Frantically, Goyahkla plunged deeper into the underbrush. Thorns scratched his skin. But he didn't care. He was sure that it was Nana who had screamed. She was still alive.

Goyahkla almost fell into a clearing. Nana was holding on to the trunk of a pine tree. She had blood on her face. Her buckskin dress had been torn.

A huge brown bear was standing in front of her. All of a sudden, the bear swiped at Nana's head. Nana screamed again. Goyahkla felt paralyzed. The bear had almost torn Nana's scalp from her head. She fell to the ground.

Goyahkla let out a bloodcurdling yell. The brown bear turned. It growled at Goyahkla.

Goyahkla ran at it with his knife. He plunged the knife over and over into the bear's stomach.

The bear kept trying to slap at Goyahkla, but Goyahkla ducked each time. The bear's sharp claws never touched him.

At last, the bear fell to the ground, dead. Goyahkla was exhausted. He wanted nothing more than to lie still and rest. But Nana had to be taken care of.

She was unconscious, but she was still breathing. Goyahkla quickly made a bed of soft pine needles and laid Nana on it. Then he used some sharp pine needles to bind Nana's scalp back onto her head.

After Goyahkla made sure Nana was comfortable, he looked around for a piece of tree bark that was curved enough to hold water. Finding it, he ran to a nearby stream, where he soaked the bark for several minutes, then filled it with water. Next, Goyahkla found some herbs he remembered his mother telling him about. They were used to heal wounds.

Goyahkla went back to where he had left Nana and made a fire. Since the piece of bark had been soaked in water, it wouldn't burn, but it would get hot enough to boil the water.

Goyahkla put the herbs in the water and boiled them until they made a thick salve. He put this salve at the edges of Nana's scalp wound. Then he cleaned Nana's other wounds. He put some of the salve on them, too.

After a while, Nana opened her eyes and groaned several times. Goyahkla whispered into her ear that he was there and that she was going to be all right. He told her to rest. Nana gave him a weak smile and then closed her eyes again.

While Nana was resting comfortably, Goyahkla skinned the huge brown bear. He cut up the meat and wrapped it inside the bear's skin. He strapped this onto the back of his pony. Then he lifted Nana onto the pony so she could rest against the skin of the bear.

When he was satisfied that Nana was safely secured, Goyahkla started down the mountain toward his village.

It was slow going. He did not want to take a chance that Nana would fall from the horse.

Several times, Goyahkla went out of his way to keep from going through undergrowth that he thought was too thick.

Finally, he reached the foot of the mountain. He headed toward the Gila River. There, he gave Nana some water to drink.

"I prayed to Usen that you would save my life, Goyahkla," Nana said. "I know that Usen has given you special powers to heal."

Goyahkla was puzzled by what Nana had just told him. He had always thought he would be a great Apache warrior. He had never thought about being a medicine man. But he had prayed to Usen that he would find Nana. Usen had shown him exactly where she was. Usen had also put the water and the right healing herbs where he would find them.

Goyahkla realized that, without thinking about it, he had acted just like an Apache medicine man. Was this how he would help his people? Goyahkla wondered. Now he was confused.

But before he could think anymore about it, people from the village had started running toward them. They were shouting, "Nana! Nana! You're alive!"

Tonight, Goyahkla decided, he would pray to Usen to show him the way that his life would go.

Although Goyahkla couldn't know it at the time, Usen would lead him to become both to the Apache people: a great warrior and a great medicine man.

Winter in the Village

Goyahkla listened to the winter wind howling outside the family tepee. He knew how cold it was. He had been outside earlier, helping his father and the other warriors feed the horses.

The snow was so deep that it was almost up to his waist. Goyahkla could not remember ever seeing so much snow. But he and his family were inside now, where it was warm.

Goyahkla loved winter. Winter was a time when the whole family would sit around the fire in the center of the tepee and talk to one another about all kinds of things. Winter brought the family closer together.

It was also a time when Taklishim would tell stories about the brave deeds of the Apache people and about Taklishlim's own hunting, raiding, and warfare.

"Tonight, I am going to tell you the story of Child of Water," Taklishim said.

Child of Water was also called Born of the Water, Goyahkla knew. He was one of the most important heroes in Apache life. Goyahkla never got tired of hearing about Child of the Water's battles with monsters.

"All life started with White Painted Woman," Taklishim began. "White Painted Woman had other children before Child of Water was born. The most important was a son called Killer of Enemies.

"During this time, White Painted Woman and Killer of Enemies lived on the earth with human beings and monsters. The monsters did not like the human beings. They would

never leave them alone so they could tend their fields or hunt the wild game.

"One of these monsters was Giant. He did terrible things. He ate some of White Painted Woman's children.

"One day, White Painted Woman decided to marry Water. They had a son together. His name was Child of Water. When Giant learned about this, he wanted to eat Child of Water, too. But White Painted Woman and Killer of Enemies hid Child of Water from him.

"Child of Water grew—"

All of a sudden, a voice from outside the tepee called, "Goyahkla?"

"Father! It's Alchise!" Goyahkla said. "May we invite him in to hear your stories?"

Taklishim smiled. "Of course, my son," he said.

Goyahkla stood up and went to the opening of the tepee. Alchise was covered with huge flakes of snow. He was grinning at Goyahkla. "I knew your father would be telling wonderful stories," he whispered. "May I come inside?"

"Of course, Alchise," Goyahkla said. "You are always welcome around our fire."

Alchise shook the snow off his clothes and followed Goyahkla to the center of the tepee. The others made room for him. Goyahkla smiled. What could be better than to have a friend over to share his family's stories?

As was the custom when guests arrived in the middle of a story, Taklishim started again from the beginning. This way, Alchise would not miss any of the exciting story.

Goyahkla listened happily to what he had already heard, for he, too, loved to hear his father's stories over and over. But he was also thinking about what to give Alchise when he left to return to his tepee. Apache custom was to give piñon nuts or pieces of dried meat to a guest to thank him for listening to stories.

Taklishim had now arrived at the point of

the story where he'd been before Alchise came.

"Child of Water grew fast. Soon, he and Killer of Enemies started hunting together. One day they came upon Giant, his family's great enemy. Child of Water used lightning to slay him.

"After this, Child of Water battled other monsters, birds, and animals, but he didn't kill all of them. He let some live so they could serve human beings.

"Now Child of Water uses the feathers of the monster eagle to make the birds that fly in the air today. Now he and his mother, White Painted Woman, help Apache girls become women by giving them instructions on what they are supposed to do during the ceremonies. Now, Killer of Enemies frees the animals from underground so they can be food for the Apache people. That is the end of the story of Child of Water."

Sounds of disappointment filled the tepee. No one wanted the stories to end.

"Tell us more, Father!" Goyahkla said.

Taklishim thought for a minute. "I will tell you the story of the Mountain People and Coyote."

"Yes! Yes!" everyone cried.

The supernatural Mountain People were also called Mountain Spirits. They lived in caves in the sacred mountains. The Mountain Spirits protected the Apache people from harm. They also healed the sick and brought happiness.

The stories about Coyote always made everyone laugh. Coyote liked to trick people. Coyote did everything wrong. If an Apache acted foolish, it was because Coyote made him do it.

By the time Taklishim finished his last story, Goyahkla had started to yawn. So had Ishton, Nah-dos-te, and Alchise. It wasn't because they was bored, Goyahkla knew. That would never happen. It was because they all felt so peaceful and content to be sitting with members of their family around a warm fire on a snowy night.

Taklishim stood. "Now I think it is time for bed," he said. "With the deep snow, it will take us twice as long to do our work tomorrow. We need plenty of rest."

Juana took down a large buckskin bag that was hanging from a notch on one of the poles of the tepee. She took out a handful of piñon nuts and handed them to Alchise. "Thank you for listening," she said.

Alchise took the nuts eagerly. "Thank you for letting me sit around your fire," he said. "I like to hear Taklishim's stories. I can see them in my head. Tonight, I will have wonderful dreams."

Goyahkla followed Alchise to the door, and the friends said good night.

Goyahkla watched his friend jump through the snow as he ran toward his family's tepee. He reminded Goyahkla of a deer.

For just a minute, Goyahkla stood and

looked at the village in the snowy moonlight. He said a short prayer to Usen. "Thank you for making me an Apache," he whispered.

Then he turned and headed to his warm buffalo blanket. Tonight, he knew, he would have wonderful dreams, too.

Young Apache Warrior

That winter was long and hard. Goyahkla's parents mostly stayed in the tepee. Taklishim had developed a bad cough. Sometimes, he didn't even want to eat. He lay on his buffalo blanket all day. Juana sat beside him. Taklishim hardly ever moved.

From time to time, Goyahkla and Alchise would leave the tepee together to hunt rabbits. That was the only meat his family had that winter. The warriors were often gone on trips south, where more and more Mexicans were beginning to move onto Apache lands, creating problems for the various tribes. So Goyahkla and Alchise had to go with some of the older men of the village to the caves in the mountain to bring down the corn, beans, and pumpkins. Because the snows were so deep, the journey took several days. By the time Goyahkla got back to his tepee, he had almost frozen to death. He lay next to his father for three days before he could force himself to get up. There was much to do. Taklishim, though, remained under the buffalo blanket.

Then one morning the sun seemed brighter, and the snow began to melt. "It's spring," Ishton cried. She was looking out the entrance of the tepee.

Goyahkla joined her. This spring was special to him. He was only fifteen now, but he planned to tell his father and the other Apache warriors that he thought he was ready to go on raids and warring expeditions. Goyahkla didn't want to wait any longer.

Goyahkla left the tepee to find Alchise. Alchise had just turned sixteen. He had suggested that they talk to the warriors together about what they wanted to do.

Alchise was in his tepee with his family. They were just finishing their morning meal. As was the custom, Goyahkla sat down at their fire and ate some stew.

It was warm, but it wasn't as good as the stew his mother made.

"How is Taklishim?" Alchise's father asked.

"He is still coughing," Goyahkla replied. He noticed that Alchise's parents exchanged worried glances. "But I think he'll get up today," Goyahkla added hurriedly.

"We will say a prayer to Usen," Alchise's mother said.

Goyahkla and Alchise finished their stew and hurried outside the tepee. The air was still crisp, but now the sun felt almost hot. All around the village the melted snow was running in little streams toward the river.

"Soon the Gila will be wide and noisy," Alchise said. "It will be hard to cross."

"But I am ready to cross it if we have to," Goyahkla told him.

Alchise grabbed Goyahkla's hands. "So am I, Brother!" he said.

Together they walked to the tepee of Cadete. Cadete met them at the entrance. "We have come to tell you that we think we are ready," Goyahkla told him. "We want to go with you on the next raiding party."

Cadete studied them both for several minutes. "That is good," he finally said. "We will soon have to fight the Mexicans and the Americans."

During the winter a shaman from the Chiricahuas had come to live in the village. A shaman was a holy man. He was a cousin of one of the people in the village. His tepee was near the banks of the Gila.

"Come. I shall take you there now," Cadete said. "The shaman will teach you the warpath words and how to act when you are raiding the Mexicans and the Americans."

Goyahkla and Alchise began following Cadete through the village. Where there wasn't snow, there was mud or water. Soon Goyahkla's moccasins were caked with mud. But this didn't matter to him. His heart was full of excitement for what was to come.

Before they reached the banks of the Gila, they could hear the roaring water. By the time they reached the shaman's tepee, the sound was so loud they could hardly hear anything else.

The shaman was waiting for them at the entrance.

How can we hear what he tells us with so much noise? Goyahkla wondered. He wanted to make sure he understood everything, so he would be accepted by the other warriors.

"Wait here!" Cadete shouted to them.

Goyahkla and Alchise stopped. Cadete went ahead and said a few words to the

137

shaman. The shaman nodded. Then he motioned for Goyahkla and Alchise to come to him.

Cadete nodded at them and left. Goyahkla and Alchise followed the shaman into his tepee.

Inside, Goyahkla could no longer hear the roar of the river. The only sound was a pounding in his ears and the labored breathing of the old shaman.

Goyahkla marveled at the inside of the shaman's tepee. In the center was the fire, but around it were bear blankets. Necklaces of bear claws were hanging from the poles of the tepee. There were baskets of all kinds along the edges.

"Please sit," the shaman instructed them.

Goyahkla and Alchise did as they were told.

"You will go on four raids with the warriors of the village," the shaman began. "If you prove to be unworthy or disobedient, the warriors will not ask you to go with them again. You will be of no worth to the village. Do you understand me?"

Goyahkla and Alchise nodded.

"You must always be on your best behavior when you go with the raiding parties. Do not be a coward. Do not be untruthful. Do not eat too much when you come back to the village," the shaman continued. "If you do these things, that will be your nature from now on."

When the shaman finished the lessons, he showed Goyahkla and Alchise how to make the clothes they would wear in battle.

First they made their war shirts. They used the softest buckskin and decorated it with beads and shell-shaped silver Mexican jewelry called conchos. Next they made their war hats. The hats had four types of feathers on them: hummingbird, oriole, quail, and eagle.

After their instructions, Goyahkla and Alchise felt ready for their first raid. It took place two days later.

Cadete had decided that the warriors of his village would join up with their Nednai brothers for a raid on Mexican farms and villages. After the long, hard winter they were in need of supplies that only the Mexicans had.

Goyahkla said good-bye to his family inside their tepee. His father was still too ill to get up. Goyahkla sat on the buffalo blanket next to his father. "I will do what I have been trained to do, Father," he whispered. "You will be proud of me."

Goyahkla was sure he saw a slight smile on his father's face. Suddenly, he felt tears in his eyes. This was not the way he had pictured his leaving on his first raid. He wanted to be by his father's side. He stood up quickly. It would not do for his father or for the rest of his family to see him crying.

"Your father will be well by the time you return, Goyahkla," his mother told him. "He is proud of you."

Goyahkla nodded. The lump in his throat kept him from saying anything.

His mother hugged him. "I will say a prayer to Usen each night before I close my eyes," she whispered. "I will pray for your safe return."

Goyahkla turned and left the tepee.

At the pony corral, Alchise was already mounted, but he was holding the reins of Goyahkla's horse. "Hurry!" he called.

Goyahkla could see that the rest of the warriors had started out of the village. This is not good, he thought. The warriors must not think I am unworthy.

Goyahkla quickly mounted his horse. He and Alchise caught up with the rear of the band, where they were supposed to ride.

As they headed south to Mexico, most of the snow had melted, but the trail was so muddy in places that it often slowed the horses.

Goyahkla tried to remember everything

the shaman had taught him. He could not turn around quickly to look behind him. He first had to glance over his shoulder. Next he had to face the sun, because this was the direction in which the Apache threw pollen. Then he could turn around.

He must always use the special warpath talk. For instance, he must never use the word "heart." He must always say "that by means of which I live."

He was not allowed to eat warm food. If his food was not cold, he would not be good with his horse.

He should not look up to the sky. If he did this, rain would come. That would not be good for the raid.

He should not laugh at anybody.

He should never speak to older warriors unless he was asked a question.

He must not say bad things about women.

He must stay awake until an older warrior said he could go to sleep.

He should show courage and never complain about anything.

After several days, the Apaches reached the Mexican border and met up with the members of the Nednai tribe. Juh rode over to Goyahkla and Alchise. He greeted them warmly. "Welcome," he said without stuttering.

"We bring you greetings," Goyahkla said.

Juh looked around. "Tell me about Ishton," he whispered. "How is she?"

"She's fine," Goyahkla said.

For a few minutes, Goyahkla was puzzled by the question. Then he realized what was happening. Juh, the boy who had stolen Ishton's basket of acorns many years before, liked Ishton. Goyahkla wondered if Juh would want to marry her when the time was right.

How strange life is, Goyahkla thought.

Over the next several days the band of Apaches raided several farms and small towns in the area.

Goyahkla and Alchise worked hard, but

they weren't allowed to fight. They carried only a bow and four blunt arrows for hunting. When the older warriors needed it, they went for water and wood. They also worked around the camp at night. The older warriors ordered them around as they wished. Goyahkla and Alchise got up early in the morning, built the fires, and cared for the horses. They cooked the meals and made the beds for the older warriors. At night, they guarded the camp.

When the Apaches had all the horses and household goods they wanted, they headed back up north. Before they reached the border, they said good-bye to the Nednais.

"I think I shall see you soon," Juh whispered to Goyahkla.

Goyahkla grinned. "We will welcome you," he said.

Over the next few months, Goyahkla and Alchise accompanied three more raiding parties. But these were not in Mexico. These raids were to the east of Goyahkla's village. More and more Americans were coming onto Apache lands.

"We must put a stop to this!" Cadete shouted to the warriors.

Goyahkla and Alchise returned their shouts of agreement.

Even though Goyahkla was still a few months short of his sixteenth birthday, he was now accepted by the other warriors as one of them. Because of this, he no longer had to stay in his tepee if he didn't want to. He was free to do what he wanted. He was free to have his own ideas. He could even marry.

Goyahkla knew he should be happy. But he wasn't. How can I be totally happy? he wondered. His father was still very ill.

Taklishim's Death

Instead of growing stronger when full spring arrived, Goyahkla's father grew weaker. The summer did not bring him health, either. When the leaves of the trees began to turn color and the sun started again toward the south, Goyahkla helped his mother move Taklishim to the north side of the tepee. They turned his face toward the east.

Once this happened, Goyahkla knew, his father didn't have many more moons to live. Inside, he began to feel anger. He wanted to talk to his father about the raids he had gone

146

on. The horses and the other things they brought back to the village would be of great use to his people. But his father no longer seemed to understand what people said to him. Still, Juana sat by his side, hardly ever leaving him.

Alchise had married and gone from the village, and Goyahkla looked forward only to a bleak autumn and winter.

Then, one day, a small band of Nednai Apaches came into the village. Juh was among them.

Goyahkla raced to embrace him. "What are you doing here?" Goyahkla asked.

"I want to marry Ishton," Juh replied. "I have come to ask your father for permission."

Goyahkla grinned big. He had been right. "I am proud that you will now be my brother, Juh," he said. "We will hunt and raid together."

Juh dismounted. Goyahkla took the reins of Juh's horse and led it to the corral. Even though Goyahkla thought of himself as a warrior of his people now, Juh was a greater warrior among the Nednais. Goyahkla was honored to lead his horse.

When they got to Goyahkla's tepee, Goyahkla found everyone in his family, except his father, standing together inside. They were dressed in their finest clothes. Someone from the Nednais' party had already told them the reason Juh was there.

Ishton blushed when she saw Juh. Juh knelt on the buffalo blanket beside Taklishim. He bent over and whispered into Taklishim's ear. Goyahkla couldn't tell for sure, but he thought he saw Taklishim slowly nod his head.

Two days later, after much dancing and feasting, Juh and Ishton were married. According to Apache custom, the husband came to live with the wife's family, so Juh and Ishton lived in a tepee that had been built next to Taklishim and Juana's.

A month later, Nah-dos-te married Concho, a warrior from the village. Concho had been living in his own tepee for almost a year, after he became a warrior. Nah-dos-te moved her belongings into Concho's tepee and set about being his wife.

Since both Ishton and Nah-dos-te were gone, Goyahkla thought no more of moving to another tepee himself. There was now plenty of room in his family's tepee. Juana also needed his help to take care of Taklishim.

Having Juh in the village lifted Goyahkla's spirits. That fall, Juh helped harvest the crops. He and Goyahkla also went hunting together. They brought back both rabbits and deer for almost everyone in the village.

Goyahkla and Juh often laughed about the time Goyahkla had waylaid Juh for stealing Ishton's basket of acorns. Only now did Goyahkla realize that even back then Juh had been in love with his sister. At the time, that was the only way Juh knew how to show it.

Even though Taklishim was growing weaker by the day, he made it through the winter,

149

which to Goyahkla didn't seem nearly as long as the one before, because there hadn't been as much snow.

But when spring came, Juh told Goyahkla one morning, "Ishton is expecting our first child. I wish to take her back to Mexico to live with my family. I want our child to grow up in the land of my boyhood."

Goyahkla was very sad. But sometimes Apache custom allowed this, if everyone in the village agreed to it. Since everyone liked Juh and Ishton very much and wanted them to be happy, they gave them permission to leave the village to live in Mexico.

"I will miss you very much, Juh," Goyahkla said.

With tears in their eyes, they embraced each other. The next morning, Ishton embraced Juana, Nah-dos-te, and Goyahkla. Then she knelt down and kissed Taklishim good-bye. "You will always be in my heart, Father," she whispered.

150

They watched from the entrance to the tepee as Juh helped Ishton onto a pony that Goyahkla had given her, and they started out of the village.

For weeks, Goyahkla moped around the village. He felt lost without Juh. Finally, he decided that he would ride south to the Nednai village and surprise Juh and Ishton with a visit. He knew it was foolish. He knew that Coyote was making him act this way. But he couldn't help it. He missed Juh and Ishton more than he ever thought he would.

But the day before he planned to leave, something happened that changed his life forever. Goyahkla was just finishing a cold piece of rabbit, when Juana suddenly stood up. "He is dead," she said.

Goyahkla stopped eating and stood up, too. He was now the head of his family. He had been trained by his grandfather and his father in what to do.

For the next two hours the people in the

village came to see Taklishim's body. When the last villager left, Goyahkla asked Skinya, now a young brave, to help him wash his father's body and then dress him in his finest clothes. Since Skinya idolized Goyahkla, he felt honored.

"I will paint his face," Nah-dos-te said.

"I will gather up all of his belongings for the journey," Juana said. She put Taklishim's bracelets, his bows and arrows, his knives, and his feathered caps onto a blanket.

"I will help you cover him," Skinya said.

Together, Goyahkla and Skinya wrapped Taklishim and his belongings in his buffalo blanket and secured it so that nothing would fall out. Outside the tepee, Cadete was holding Taklishim's favorite horse. Several warriors of the village lifted Taklishim's body and tied it carefully onto the horse.

Goyahkla took the reins of his father's horse. He began leading the horse out of the village. Juana and Nah-dos-te walked behind

him. They were crying and wailing according to Apache custom.

Only Taklishim's family and closest friends were allowed to attend the burial. Goyahkla led Taklishim's horse toward the Gila River, where they all crossed together. Once on the other side, they started up the mountain toward the cave where Taklishim and Goyahkla had once hidden their food.

"It is a good cave," Goyahkla had told Juana. "Father will be happy there."

Halfway up the mountain, thick clouds surrounded them. The winds swept down from the north and swirled around them. But the Mountain Spirits held back the rain. Finally, they reached the cave. "Skinya, help me lift my father from his horse," Goyahkla said.

Together, Goyahkla and Skinya carried Taklishim's body into the cave. They opened the buffalo blanket. Juana and Nah-dos-te arranged Taklishim's body so he appeared to be sleeping. They placed his belongings close to him so he would be able to reach them on his long journey. When they were finished, Goyahkla said, "It is time to seal the cave."

The members of the burial party looked for big rocks. They stacked them at the entrance until they reached the top. Then they coated the rocks with mud so that the entrance would be hidden.

Goyahkla, Juana, and Nah-dos-te took one last look at where Taklishim was buried. They would never visit this place again. They would never mention Taklishim's name again, either. That was Apache custom.

"It is time to go back down the mountain," Goyahkla said. He helped Juana and Nah-dos-te onto horses. "There is much to be done in our village."

As they started back down the mountain, Goyahkla had visions of all the many wonderful things that had happened to him in the years he had been alive. He had had a very happy childhood. But he knew that when they reached the village again, he would begin a new life.

Geronimo!

Not too long after Taklishim's death, Juana told Goyahkla that she, too, wanted to go visit Ishton and her friends among the Nednais in Mexico. While they were there, Goyahkla met the woman who would become his wife. Her name was Alope. But Goyahkla didn't want to live in Mexico forever, so after their marriage, the Nednais allowed them to return to the Bedonkohe village near the Gila River.

Over the next few years, Goyahkla and Alope had three children. One day, Juana again asked Goyahkla to take her south to Mexico to see her family and friends. They were all very excited. They would not only enjoy the visit but they would also be able to exchange their furs and hides for some of the colorful clothing in the Mexican markets.

On their way, they made a large wickiup camp outside the town of Janos. The men went into town for supplies. While they were gone, the Mexicans attacked the wickiups. Almost everyone was killed—including Goyahkla's wife, his children, and his mother.

What was left of the Apache band went back to their village near the Gila River. Goyahkla burned his tepee and everything in it. He crawled on his hands and knees to the top of a nearby mountain. He prayed to Usen. Usen told him to avenge the death of all Apaches. He told Goyahkla that no gun would ever kill him.

Over the next few years, Goyahkla and other Apache warriors fought the Mexicans and the Americans. During one battle, the Mexicans started praying to Saint Jerome to save them from Goyahkla. To the Apaches, it sounded like they were saying "Geronimo." From that day on, Goyahkla went by the name Geronimo.

The Americans and Apaches tried several times to make peace. But the treaties were always broken—sometimes by the Americans and sometimes by the Apaches.

On several occasions, American troops captured Geronimo. They sent him to reservations they had established in what would become Arizona and New Mexico. But Geronimo always managed to escape.

Soon, Geronimo and his small band were the only Apaches the American troops hadn't captured. Time and again they would be captured, but each time they would escape, until 1886, when they surrendered to the Americans for good. Geronimo would escape no more.

Prisoner of War

After Geronimo surrendered to the Americans, he and several hundred other Apaches were put on a train to Florida. They were miserable. They weren't used to such a humid climate. It was nothing like the dry air of Arizona and New Mexico. Many people died.

From Florida, the Apaches were taken to Alabama. Geronimo kept asking the United States government to send his people to a healthy place to live.

Finally, the Comanche and Kiowa Indians in Oklahoma said they would give the Apaches part of their land. So Geronimo and his people moved to Fort Sill, Oklahoma.

At first, the white people in Oklahoma were nervous about having Geronimo living among them. They still remembered when he had been a warrior in Arizona and New Mexico. But then some businessmen had an idea: They could put Geronimo on display. They were sure that lots of people would pay money to come see this fierce warrior. They were right.

These businessmen took Geronimo around the country. He appeared at fairs and carnivals. The businessmen made money. But so did Geronimo. He sold pictures of himself for twenty-five cents. In 1904, he appeared at the World's Fair in St. Louis, Missouri. The next year, he rode in the inauguration parade of President Theodore Roosevelt.

Geronimo eventually remarried and spent the last years of his life with his new family at Fort Sill. He tended his gardens, and he told his grandchildren about what life was like when he was a small boy. He died in 1909. He was buried in one of the Apache cemeteries at Fort Sill.

During World War II, American paratroopers, to show their bravery, started yelling "Geronimo" when they parachuted out of airplanes. In doing this, they were also paying homage to one of the bravest figures in American history.

People of all races still come daily to Geronimo's grave to pay their respects to this great warrior who fought to make sure that the Apaches had a land that was perfect for them.

Childhood of Famous Americans

One of the most popular series ever published for young Americans, these classics have been praised alike by parents, teachers, and librarians. With these lively, inspiring, fictionalized biographies—easily read by children of eight and up—today's youngster is swept right into history.

ABIGAIL ADAMS   JOHN ADAMS   LOUISA MAY ALCOTT
SUSAN B. ANTHONY   NEIL ARMSTRONG   CRISPUS ATTUCKS
CLARA BARTON   ELIZABETH BLACKWELL   DANIEL BOONE
BUFFALO BILL   ROBERTO CLEMENTE   DAVY CROCKETT   JOE
DIMAGGIO   WALT DISNEY   AMELIA EARHART   THOMAS A.
EDISON   ALBERT EINSTEIN   HENRY FORD   BENJAMIN
FRANKLIN   LOU GEHRIG   GERONIMO   ALTHEA GIBSON
JOHN GLENN   JIM HENSON   HARRY HOUDINI   LANGSTON
HUGHES   ANDREW JACKSON   MAHALIA JACKSON   THOMAS
JEFFERSON   HELEN KELLER   JOHN FITZGERALD KENNEDY
MARTIN LUTHER KING JR.   ROBERT E. LEE   MERIWETHER
LEWIS   ABRAHAM LINCOLN   MARY TODD LINCOLN
THURGOOD MARSHALL   JOHN MUIR   ANNIE OAKLEY
JACQUELINE KENNEDY ONASSIS   ROSA PARKS   MOLLY
PITCHER   POCAHONTAS   RONALD REAGAN   PAUL REVERE
JACKIE ROBINSON   KNUTE ROCKNE   MR. ROGERS
ELEANOR ROOSEVELT   FRANKLIN DELANO ROOSEVELT
TEDDY ROOSEVELT   BETSY ROSS   WILMA RUDOLPH   BABE
RUTH   SACAGAWEA   SITTING BULL   JIM THORPE   HARRY S.
TRUMAN   SOJOURNER TRUTH   HARRIET TUBMAN   MARK
TWAIN   GEORGE WASHINGTON   MARTHA WASHINGTON
LAURA INGALLS WILDER   WILBUR AND ORVILLE WRIGHT

Collect them all!